the CRiTTeR club

 Marion Takes Charge

by Callie Barkley 💙 illustrated by Marsha Riti

LITTLE SIMON

New York London Toronto Sydney New Delhi

 LITTLE SIMON

An imprint of Simon & Schuster Children's Publishing Division • 1230 Avenue of the Americas, New York, New York 10020 • First Little Simon hardcover edition September 2015 • Copyright © 2015 by Simon & Schuster, Inc. All rights reserved, including the right of reproduction in whole or in part in any form. LITTLE SIMON is a registered trademark of Simon & Schuster, Inc., and associated colophon is a trademark of Simon & Schuster, Inc. For information about special discounts for bulk purchases, please contact Simon & Schuster Special Sales at 1-866-506-1949 or business@simonandschuster.com. The Simon & Schuster Speakers Bureau can bring authors to your live event. For more information or to book an event contact the Simon & Schuster Speakers Bureau at 1-866-248-3049 or visit our website at www.simonspeakers.com. Designed by Laura Roode. The text of this book was set in ITC Stone Informal Std.

Manufactured in the United States of America 0815 FFG 10 9 8 7 6 5 4 3 2 1

Library of Congress Cataloging-in-Publication Data

Barkley, Callie. Marion takes charge / by Callie Barkley ; illustrated by Marsha Riti. — First Little Simon paperback edition. pages cm. — (Critter Club ; #12)

Summary: When Marion finally gets the chance to babysit her little sister, she finds that the task is harder than she expected, especially when she gets called to the Critter Club to help with a stray cat and must bring Gabby along. [1. Babysitters—Fiction. 2. Sisters—Fiction. 3. Clubs—Fiction. 4. Animal shelters—Fiction.] I. Riti, Marsha, illustrator. II. Title. PZ7.B250585Maw 2015 [Fic]—dc23 2014049484

ISBN 978-1-4814-2409-7 (hc)

ISBN 978-1-4814-2408-0 (pbk)

ISBN 978-1-4814-2410-3 (eBook)

Table of Contents

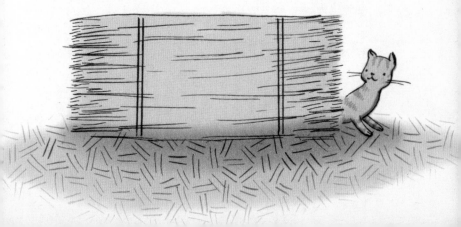

Chapter 1

Marion, the Big Sister

"Here, Gabby," Marion Ballard said to her little sister. "I'll do that for you."

"No, I can do it!" Gabby replied. She was at the front door, tying her shoes. Marion thought she was doing it way too slowly.

Mrs. Ballard was waiting in the car. Marion checked her watch. It

was 8:35. School started at 8:45, and the drive was eight minutes long. If they didn't get going, they'd be late!

Finally, Gabby was ready. They rushed outside.

Phew! thought Marion as her mom backed out of the driveway.

Marion made sure she had everything. She had her lunch box.

She had her sneakers for gym. She peeked inside her homework folder. Yep, she had her homework.

"Do you have your lunch, Gabby?" Marion asked her sister.

Gabby nodded. "Your home-work?" Marion said.

Gabby nodded again. She was in kindergarten. She usually had a short math work sheet and some reading homework.

"Your reading folder?" Marion asked.

Gabby's eyes went wide in alarm. "I forgot to read the new book in my reading folder!"

Marion looked out the car window. They still had a few minutes before they got to school. "Want to read it together now?" Marion asked.

Gabby smiled and nodded. She pulled out the book. It was called *My Bike*.

Marion held the book and turned the pages as Gabby read. She helped Gabby with words she didn't know.

It was a short book, and they finished just as Mrs. Ballard pulled up to the school.

"Thanks, Marion!" said Gabby, tucking her book into her backpack.

Marion smiled. She was glad she helped Gabby start her day off right.

Mrs. Ballard helped Marion and Gabby out of the car.

She gave Gabby a kiss on her

head. "Have a great day!" she said as Gabby walked off toward the school entrance. Then she looked at Marion.

"That was great, the way you helped your sister just now," said

Mrs. Ballard proudly. "In fact, I have a question for you. You know how you've always wanted to babysit Gabby?"

Marion nodded. It was true. She *was* always begging her parents to babysit.

"Well," said her mom with a smile, "Dad and I are having a party for some friends on Saturday. We'll be home the whole time. But I'm wondering . . . will you be in charge of watching Gabby during the party?"

Marion gasped. "Yes!" she cried. She jumped up and down with excitement. Her parents had always told her she was too young to baby-sit. But now they thought she was ready for the responsibility!

"Thank you, Mom!" Marion cried, hugging her mother. "Thank you, thank you, thank you!"

Then Marion hurried into school. She couldn't wait to tell her best friends the big news!

Chapter 2

The Club's New Critter

Marion had gym later that morning. It was her first chance to talk to Amy, Liz, and Ellie.

"They're going to let me babysit!" Marion exclaimed. She'd told them about her parents' party. "I'm going to watch Gabby upstairs while they have their party downstairs."

The girls were standing in a

circle. They were playing Hot Potato with a ball. When the gym teacher turned off the music, whoever was holding the ball was out.

Marion tossed the ball to Liz.

"Stewart babysat me one time," Liz said. Stewart was Liz's big brother. "But I think *I* should have been in charge. He was going to make a pizza bagel in the slice toaster. I stopped him.

That would have been a mess!"

Liz threw the ball to Ellie.

Ellie shook her head. "I would never want to babysit Toby," she said. Toby was Ellie's little brother. "He wears me out even when I'm not in charge!"

Ellie tossed the ball to Amy.

"I think I'm better at babysitting animals than kids," Amy said. Amy's mom, Dr. Purvis, was a veterinarian. She also helped the girls run their animal rescue shelter, The Critter Club.

Just then the music stopped. Marion, Ellie, and Liz looked at Amy.

"I know, I know," Amy said. "I'm out."

Amy stepped to one side. The music came back on. The girls continued playing. Ellie threw the ball to Liz.

"Oh, guess what?" Amy said from the sidelines. "My mom found a stray cat yesterday!" Liz threw the ball to Marion as Amy went on. "She said she seemed really weak at first," Amy said. "But my mom gave her some food and a couple

of shots. She's doing a lot better. She might be ready to come to The Critter Club by Friday!"

"Then we can figure out if she has a home . . . or if she needs one!" Marion said happily.

The music stopped. Marion still

had the ball. Her smile faded—
but only for a second. She was too
excited about the cat.

Marion *loved* cats. Her own kitten, Ollie, had been a guest at The Critter Club once. He had been in a litter born to a stray mama cat. The girls had found homes for all the other kittens. But Marion hadn't wanted to say good-bye to Ollie. So her family had adopted him!

Marion couldn't wait to meet the latest Critter Club cat on Friday. And then she'd get to babysit Gabby on Saturday!

This is going to be the best weekend ever! she thought.

Chapter 3

How to Calm a Cat

On Friday after school, Marion's dad gave her a ride to Ms. Sullivan's house. She hurried into the barn, The Critter Club headquarters. Liz, Ellie, Amy, and Dr. Purvis were there.

They'd had two animal guests for the last week. One was an iguana they were pet-sitting for a family on

vacation. The other was a mouse. His last owner was allergic to him. The girls were trying to find him a new home.

When Marion walked in, her friends were gathered around a pet crate on a table. Inside, all snuggled up, was a tabby cat with orange and white stripes.

"Girls, meet our new friend," Dr. Purvis said. She opened the door of the crate and stepped back. "She might be shy at first. Let her come out when she's ready."

While they waited, they talked about the cat's name. "She didn't have a collar," Dr. Purvis pointed out. "But it's possible she has an owner and a name already."

"How about we just call her 'Tabby' for now?" Liz suggested. All the girls agreed.

Finally, Tabby crept toward the crate's open door. She stuck her head out cautiously. Then, slowly, she stepped out.

Ellie cooed in her sweetest voice: "Hello there, kitty." She reached out to pick her up. But Tabby drew back and hissed!

"Whoa!" Ellie cried.

Dr. Purvis put a hand on Ellie's shoulder. "Don't take it personally," she said. "She's nervous. Let's not pick her up just yet."

Amy spoke up. "Maybe she wants to smell us first?" Amy rested her hand on the table a few feet from Tabby. But the cat turned away. "I

guess not!" Amy said with a shrug.

Dr. Purvis frowned. "Hmm. She probably just needs to get used to it here. Let's let her explore. Meanwhile, we can get her room ready."

Tabby's "room" was the empty horse stall at the back of the barn. It had four walls, a door, and plenty of space inside.

"This is perfect," said Liz. "When we're here, we can let her roam around. And when we're not, we can close the door. That way, she won't try to get into the other pets' cages."

Together, the girls worked to make the stall cozy. They piled old blankets in one corner.

"That's a nice sleeping spot," said Ellie.

Amy pulled a few cat toys out of her backpack. "I brought these from the clinic."

Marion set up a litter box in a little alcove. "She'll be needing this for sure," she said.

Just then Marion noticed her shoe was untied. She sat down on the floor to tie it. As she was making the double knot, she heard a soft *mew* at her side. Marion turned her head. Tabby was at her elbow, looking up at her. Marion didn't move. She wanted to give Tabby some time to decide what *she* wanted.

Slowly, Tabby came around in front of Marion. She stepped into Marion's lap. Then she lay down and put her chin on Marion's leg.

Marion looked up. Amy, Ellie, Liz, and Dr. Purvis were staring at Tabby in shock.

Then Dr. Purvis smiled. "Well," she said, "it looks like someone has made a friend."

Chapter 4

Sister Sitter

Marion jumped out of bed early on Saturday morning. *Today I'm not just Gabby's sister. I'm Gabby's babysitter!* she thought.

She stood in front of her closet. Which of her outfits would make her look the most responsible? Marion picked out a long-sleeved shirt, a sweater, a corduroy skirt, and leggings. She was comfy, warm, and ready for anything.

Then Marion went to brush her teeth in the bathroom. She even flossed after. *Responsible people definitely floss,* she thought.

Down in the kitchen, Marion's parents had made breakfast. Gabby was at the table, eating her pancakes.

"Hungry?" Mrs. Ballard asked Marion.

Marion nodded and sat down.

Eating a good breakfast is very responsible, she thought. *It's the most important meal of the day!*

Mrs. Ballard gave Marion a plate of pancakes and berries. She poured her a glass of juice. Then

she sat down with the girls.

"So, the party isn't until this afternoon," Mrs. Ballard said. "But Dad and I have lots to do to get the house ready. Can you watch Gabby while we're setting things up?"

Marion nodded. "No problem!" she exclaimed. "Don't worry about us. I've got everything under control!"

Marion ran up to her room. She came back with her notebook. "I made a list last night," she explained. "It's a whole bunch of activities for us to do today!"

Mrs. Ballard smiled at both Marion and Gabby. "Okay, then!"

she said. "We will be in the living room. We'll be busy, but we're here if you need us."

Then she walked out of the room, leaving Marion and Gabby alone at the table. Gabby sat there quietly, staring at Marion.

Marion eyed Gabby's glass. "Do you need more juice?" Marion asked.

Gabby shook her head no. "No, thanks," she replied.

Marion peeked over at Gabby's plate. There was almost a whole pancake left.

"Aren't you going to finish?" Marion asked.

Gabby shrugged. "I'm full."

"You should finish," Marion said in her most adult voice. "You need food to keep your energy up!"

Gabby crossed her arms in front of her. She seemed to have her mind made up.

Marion ate her breakfast quickly.

Then she asked Gabby if she wanted to see the activities list.

"Okay!" Gabby replied excitedly.

Marion pointed at number one on the list. "Clean Gabby's room!"

Gabby's smile disappeared. "Clean my room?" she repeated. "That's no fun!"

1. clean Gabby's room
2. play a board game
3. drawing
4. play outside
5. take a bath

Marion shrugged. "But your room really needs it," she said, standing up from the table. "Come on. I'll help you."

Gabby groaned.

Marion led the way up the stairs. "I know this isn't the best thing on the list," she called over her shoulder, "but soon we'll be done. Then

we can get to the next activity: playing a board game!"

Marion got to the top step. She turned around, adding, "That sounds fun, right?"

Gabby wasn't there. She hadn't followed Marion. Marion could see her downstairs, still at the kitchen table.

Marion took a deep breath. *Maybe this is going to be harder than I thought.*

Chapter 5

A Call for Help

It took longer than Marion expected to clean Gabby's room. Maybe it was because only Marion was really cleaning up. Every time she looked over, Gabby was *playing* with a toy instead of putting it away.

Finally, Marion looked around and sighed. "Good enough." She and Gabby went down to the

playroom. They stood in front of the game closet. "What should we play?" Marion asked.

Gabby answered right away. "Candy Land!"

Ugh, thought Marion. She had played Candy Land a zillion times! "How about Scrabble Junior?" Marion tried. It would help her get ready for the spelling test next week.

Gabby pouted and said, "I really, really, *really* want to play Candy Land."

Marion sighed. "Okay. Candy Land it is." She was trying hard to be a good babysitter.

Gabby grabbed the green game piece. It was Marion's favorite from when she was little. But Marion let Gabby take it. Marion took red instead.

In the middle of the game, Gabby drew a card that made her go back lots of spaces. She wanted to pick again. Marion let her.

Marion was on a lucky streak. She was out in front. Then she picked the ice-cream card and got to skip even farther ahead. She was so close to the candy castle!

"I don't want to play anymore,"
Gabby said suddenly.

"What?" Marion cried. "I let you

pick the game. I let you have the green piece. I let you have a do-over. Now you're quitting?"

Gabby turned her back to Marion.

Marion was frustrated. She tried to calm down as she walked to the hall closet. She got out the big marker box for their next activity—drawing. So far, babysitting Gabby was *not much fun*!

Marion was in the hall when the phone rang. She heard her dad pick up in the living room. "Oh, hi, Ellie!" he said.

Marion perked up at the sound of Ellie's name. She poked her head in the living room. Her dad handed her the phone.

"Hey!" said Ellie on the other end. "I'm at Ms. Sullivan's house. Amy, Liz, and I got here an hour ago. Tabby wasn't in her room, and we still can't find her. We've looked everywhere!"

"Oh, no!" said Marion.

"I know!" said Ellie. "So we were

thinking. . . . Tabby really seemed to like you yesterday. Maybe she'd come if *you* called. Is there any way you could come over?"

Marion opened her mouth to say, "Yes!" After all, her friends needed her help. But she couldn't. She'd been wanting to babysit Gabby for *forever*, and she'd promised her parents she would. She needed to prove she could handle it.

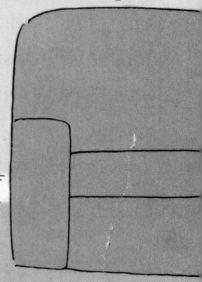

63

Marion to the Rescue

Marion told Ellie she would come as soon as the party was over. "I'm sorry I can't come sooner," she said sadly.

Ellie said she understood. Marion wished she could be in two places at once.

Her dad heard her hang up the phone. "What's up?" he asked.

Marion explained that Tabby was missing and her friends needed her help. "But I know you need me here to watch Gabby."

As the words came out, Marion gasped. "Or maybe you don't need me *here*!" she cried.

Her dad looked confused.

"Dad," said Marion, "could I take Gabby with me to The Critter Club? She's always wanted to come!"

Mr. Ballard thought it over. "I don't see why not," he replied.

He called Ms. Sullivan to make sure she would be there with the girls. When he hung up, he gave Marion a thumbs-up. "I'll drive you both over," he said. "And I'll pick you up at three, when the party is over. Sound good?"

"Great!" Marion exclaimed.

She ran to the playroom to tell Gabby, who was even more excited than Marion was.

"You can help us find Tabby!" Marion told her. Gabby stood up proudly—all ready for her mission.

Marion tried to get Gabby to put

on a sweater. "Sometimes it's chilly
in the barn," Marion warned. But
Gabby didn't want to wear it.

Marion sighed. They hurried
into Mr. Ballard's car and rode over
to The Critter Club.

Ellie, Amy, and Liz ran out to

meet them when they got there. "We're so glad you're here!" Ellie cried.

"Hi, Gabby," Amy said kindly. "Are you going to help us too?"

"Yep!" Gabby exclaimed.

They all went into the barn. Liz showed Gabby where Tabby's room was. "This is where we expected her to be this morning," she said.

Amy pointed toward the litter box. Behind it, in a dark corner of

the room, there was a small hole in the wall. "We think maybe she squeezed out through there," Amy said.

"We're hoping she's still in the barn somewhere," Ellie added. "If she got outside, she could be *anywhere*!"

Marion tried calling. "Here, Tabby, Tabby. Here, kitty!"

She moved around the barn. Gabby followed her. Meanwhile, the others fanned out in all directions. They peeked in corners, under tables, and in the supply closet.

"Here, Tabby!" Marion called a little louder. "Where are you? Come out, Tabby!"

They kept at it for nearly fifteen minutes. Marion called and called until her voice sounded tired.

But there was no sign of Tabby anywhere in the barn.

Marion sat down on a hay bale in the corner. Gabby sat next to her. Marion's shoulders slumped. She looked at her friends. "I guess I haven't been any help at all!" she said.

Just then, from behind the hay bale, Tabby crept out silently. The girls all saw her, but no one spoke or moved. They just watched as Tabby padded slowly toward Marion. The cat climbed up into her lap. She sat down. And then she started to purr.

Chapter 7

Gabby Meets Tabby

Marion looked over at Ellie, Amy, and Liz. They were all smiling.

"It worked!" Amy whispered.

Liz and Ellie cheered silently. No one wanted to startle Tabby.

But Gabby didn't realize this. She was too excited to meet Tabby for the first time. "TAB-by! I'm GAB-by!" she shrieked, and leaned over eagerly to pet the cat.

Tabby's head jerked up. Her back arched. But Gabby didn't notice. She kept petting her fur from tail to head—the *wrong* way. Suddenly, Tabby screeched. *Rawrrrr!* She shot out of Marion's lap and was gone

behind the hay
again.

"Gabby!"
Marion snapped.
"Look what you did!"

Gabby froze, startled
by Marion's tone. Her brow wrinkled
and her chin trembled. Marion had
seen that look many times. It usually happened right before Gabby
started to cry.

Marion felt bad.
She reached out
for Gabby's arm.
"Oh, Gabby, I'm

sorry," Marion said. She tried to speak extra gently. "It's okay. It's just . . . Tabby is very jumpy. And most cats prefer to be pet the *other* way—from their heads toward their tails."

"But you didn't know that," said Ellie kindly. She and Liz and Amy came over. Ellie patted Gabby on the back.

"Yeah, don't worry," said Liz. "Now we know where Tabby is. We'll get her to come out again."

"Hey! I have an idea," Amy said to Gabby. "Do you want to meet the other animals staying here?"

A tiny smile lit up Gabby's face. She nodded. Amy and Ellie led her over to the iguana's terrarium and the mouse's cage. Meanwhile, Marion and Liz tried to get Tabby to come out of hiding again.

Soon, the barn was peaceful. Tabby was lapping milk from a bowl. The iguana and the mouse had also been fed. They'd cleaned out Tabby's litter box. The girls had written an ad to put in next week's newspaper. The headline read:

Cute Gray Mouse Needs a Home

Contact The Critter Club

CUTE GRAY
MOUSE NEEDS
A HOME. Then they had made some
flyers to put up around town. They
planned to put them up next week.

"What should we do now?"
Marion asked. "My dad isn't coming

to get us until three o'clock." They had all afternoon to spend at The Critter Club.

The girls thought it over. "Want to play Three, Two, One, Draw?" Ellie suggested.

"Yeah!" the others replied at once.

The girls kept the game in the barn's supply closet. They loved it—it was like a drawing version of charades. One person drew, and her

teammates tried to guess what she was drawing. Sometimes they just played a short speed round. Other times, they played the full-length game.

Liz started to set up the game. "Wait," she

said. "There are five of us. We won't have even teams."

The girls all thought it over.

"I have an idea," said Marion suddenly. "Why don't Gabby and I be on one team. You three can be on the other."

Marion winked at Gabby. She

wanted Gabby to know she wasn't mad at her.

Gabby gave a huge smile. "Let's play!" she said.

Animals Everywhere!

Just as they started the game, Ms. Sullivan stuck her head into the barn.

"Hello in here!" she said cheerfully. "I have a favor to ask. I made a big batch of cookie dough. I need to roll it out and cut the cookies. It sure would go faster if I had a few helpers!" She flashed a sweet smile.

"And I'm willing to pay in fresh-baked cookies!"

All of the girls eagerly volunteered. But then Marion looked down at Tabby.

"Gabby," she said, "maybe you and I should stay here to

keep an eye on Tabby."

Amy agreed. "That's probably a good idea," she said. "But don't worry. We'll bring you each a cookie!"

Amy, Liz, and Ellie went off with Ms. Sullivan. Marion and Gabby were left alone in the barn with the animals.

Tabby had finished her milk. She curled up next to Marion. She licked her paws and rubbed her face to clean herself. She looked as calm as could be. Marion reached out and pet Tabby very lightly.

Tabby didn't hiss. She didn't flinch. She put her head down and closed her eyes.

"Look!" Marion whispered to Gabby. "I think she's really settling in, finally."

Gabby didn't answer. She was standing by the mouse cage with her back to Marion.

"Gabby?" Marion said. "What are you—?"

Marion didn't finish her question. Suddenly, Tabby was on her feet, bolting toward the mouse cage. At the same moment, Gabby let out a shriek as a small streak of gray fur scurried across the table.

The mouse was loose! And Tabby was chasing it!

Gabby shrieked again as Tabby ran between her legs. Startled and off balance, Gabby stumbled backward. She bumped into the table behind her. On the tabletop, the iguana terrarium teetered and fell over. The mesh lid came off.

"Oh, no!" cried Marion. She ran toward the terrarium. She had to

get the lid back on—quickly!

But it was too late.

The iguana scrambled out just as Marion got there.

It scurried across the table, down a table leg, and across the floor.

Marion didn't know which way to go first! Everything was completely out of control!

"Tabby! I mean, *Gabby*!" she shouted frantically. "Follow that iguana! I'll try to save the mouse!

Come back here, Gabby! I mean *Tabby*!"

But Gabby just stood frozen to her spot, shrieking louder and louder. Ms. Sullivan and the girls must have heard her from the house. Suddenly they rushed into the barn.

Working together, Amy and Liz cornered

the iguana. They got him back into the terrarium and put the lid on.

Marion managed to catch up to Tabby. She held on to the cat. Meanwhile, Ms. Sullivan and Ellie slowly coaxed the mouse out from the supply closet.

Before long, all the animals were back where they were supposed to be. Everyone breathed a sigh of relief.

Everyone, that is, except for Marion. She was completely worn out. She turned and marched over to Gabby.

"What were you *thinking?*"

Marion yelled. "You *weren't* think-ing, were you?"

Instantly, Gabby burst into tears. She turned and ran out of the barn.

Sisterly Love

Marion sighed. No one needed to tell her. She knew she had sounded really harsh. *Gabby must have felt terrible about letting the animals out. And I just made her feel even worse,* Marion thought.

Marion went outside. Gabby was sitting under the big tree in Ms. Sullivan's backyard. Her head

107

was buried in her hands.

Marion sat down next to her. She put her arm around her little sister.

"I'm so sorry, Gabby," Marion said. "I shouldn't have yelled at you."

Gabby looked up at Marion. "I wasn't trying to let the mouse out," Gabby sobbed. "I just wanted to pet him the way you were petting Tabby. It just . . . it just happened so fast!"

"I know," said Marion. "Animals don't always do what we expect. It's hard work taking care of them."

She paused, thinking about her day with Gabby so far. "It's hard work taking care of people, too."

They sat under the tree for a little while. Marion told Gabby about the times *she* had messed up at The Critter Club. "Like when Ollie and his brothers and sisters were here,"

Marion told her. "I was trying to feed one of them from a bottle. Instead, I spilled milk all over the kitten!"

Gabby smiled. She giggled, imagining Marion making a mess.

Mew.

Marion and Gabby looked up. There was Tabby, standing a few feet away in the grass. Marion crisscrossed her legs to make a lap for Tabby to climb into.

But instead, Tabby stepped

lightly into Gabby's lap. She sat down and put her head on Gabby's leg. Gabby gasped in surprise.

"She likes you, too!" Marion cried. Gabby beamed.

The sisters sat for a few more

minutes and then returned to the barn. Soon, all the girls were deep into their game of Three, Two, One, Draw. Marion and Gabby were winning. They made a fantastic team.

"It's no fair!" Ellie said. "Gabby makes two little squiggles on the paper. And just like that, you know it's a horse?"

Liz held up one of the drawings Marion had made. "And Gabby! How did you get 'helicopter' from *this*?"

Gabby shrugged and looked at Marion. The two of them burst out laughing.

"What can we say?" Marion said between giggles. "We know each other very well!" She put her arm around Gabby. Just then Gabby shivered. "Are you cold?" Marion asked her.

Gabby shrugged. "A little," she admitted.

I knew it! Marion thought. *I told her she should have brought a sweater.*

But Marion didn't say that to Gabby. Instead, she took off her sweater. She wrapped it around Gabby's shoulders. "Here. You can wear mine for a little while."

"Thanks," Gabby said.

Marion smiled. Then a thought popped into her mind. As much

as she had wanted the chance to babysit, she didn't really *need* to be Gabby's sitter. Because being Gabby's *sister* was a lot more fun.

Read on for a sneak peek at
the next Critter Club book:

#13

Amy Is a
Little Bit Chicken

the CRiTTeR club

#13

Amy Is a
Little Bit
Chicken

by Callie Barkley · illustrated by Tracy Bishop

Cluck, cluck, baaawk! A hen came wandering into the barn. Two more followed right behind her.

The chickens had arrived the day before. They had been wandering around downtown Santa Vista. They even walked into the road, stopping traffic! No one knew where they'd come from. And no one knew what to do!

Then Ms. Sullivan happened to pass by. She knew a place the chickens could stay while their owner was found: The Critter Club!

Already the girls had learned a lot about keeping chickens. For starters, they needed a coop, or henhouse. Luckily Ms. Sullivan's neighbors offered to help. Mr. Mack was a farmer and Mrs. Mack was a carpenter. Together, they made the perfect coop-building team.

The girls went outside to see how it was coming along. Behind the barn, Mrs. Mack was hammering a shingle onto the coop roof.

"Wow, it's almost done!" Ellie exclaimed.

"We have a few more things to add inside," said Mrs. Mack. "Let's try to get them inside of it."

Amy tried luring them with chicken feed. But when she tossed some toward them, the hens ran away from it.

"It seems like they're afraid of *everything*," Amy said to Mr. Mack.

He smiled. "Chickens sometimes are kind of . . . chicken."

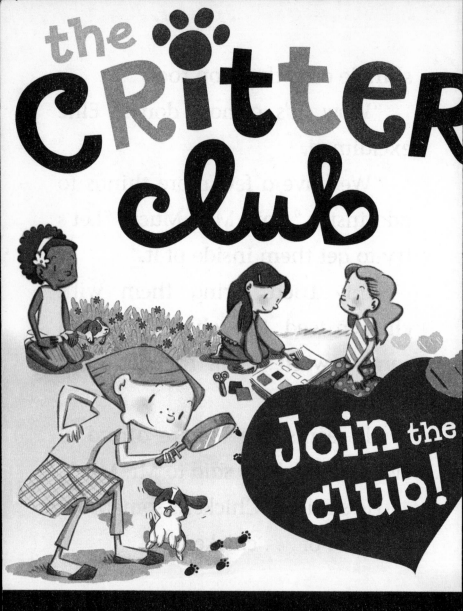